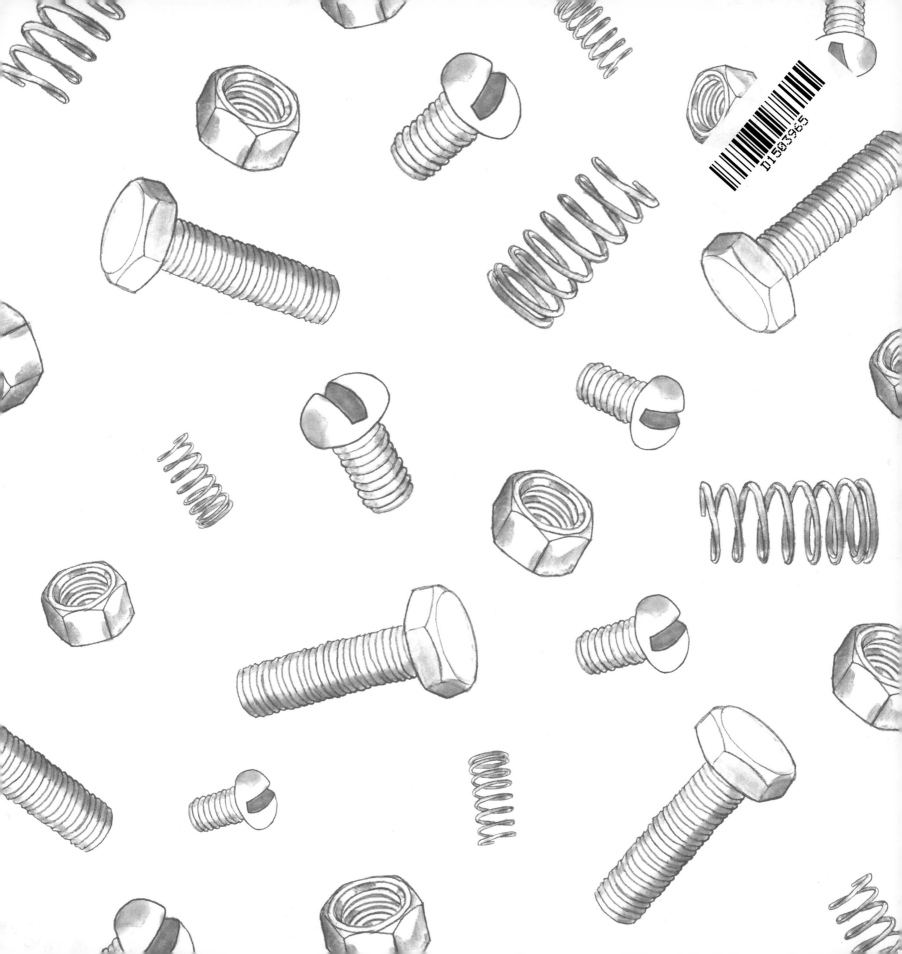

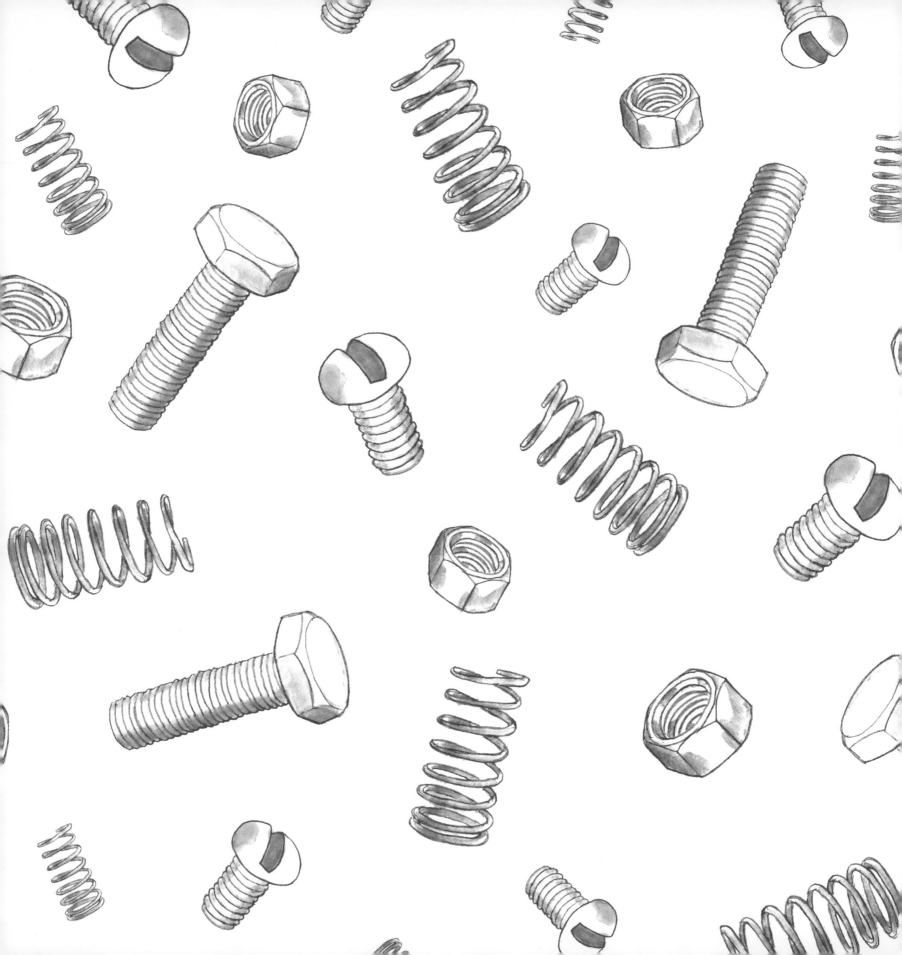

BETTY BUILDS IT

Julie Hampton

WEST
MARGIN
PRESS

For Max, who explained why the wind car belongs in the junk pile.

Text and Illustrations © 2019 by Julie Hampton

Edited by Michelle McCann

Library of Congress Cataloging-in-Publication Data is on file.

ISBN 9781513262321 (hardbound)
ISBN 9781513262338 (e-book)

Printed in China
22 21 20 19 1 2 3 4 5

Published by West Margin Press®

**WEST
MARGIN
PRESS**
WestMarginPress.com

Proudly distributed by Ingram Publisher Services

WEST MARGIN PRESS
Publishing Director: Jennifer Newens
Marketing Manager: Angela Zbornik
Editor: Olivia Ngai
Design & Production: Rachel Lopez Metzger

Betty could build just about anything.

Her home was a fabulous workshop full of tools and spare parts.

She shared her home with a parental unit

and a baby brother, Toby,
who couldn't do much.

She longed for a friend who could
do the same things she liked to do:

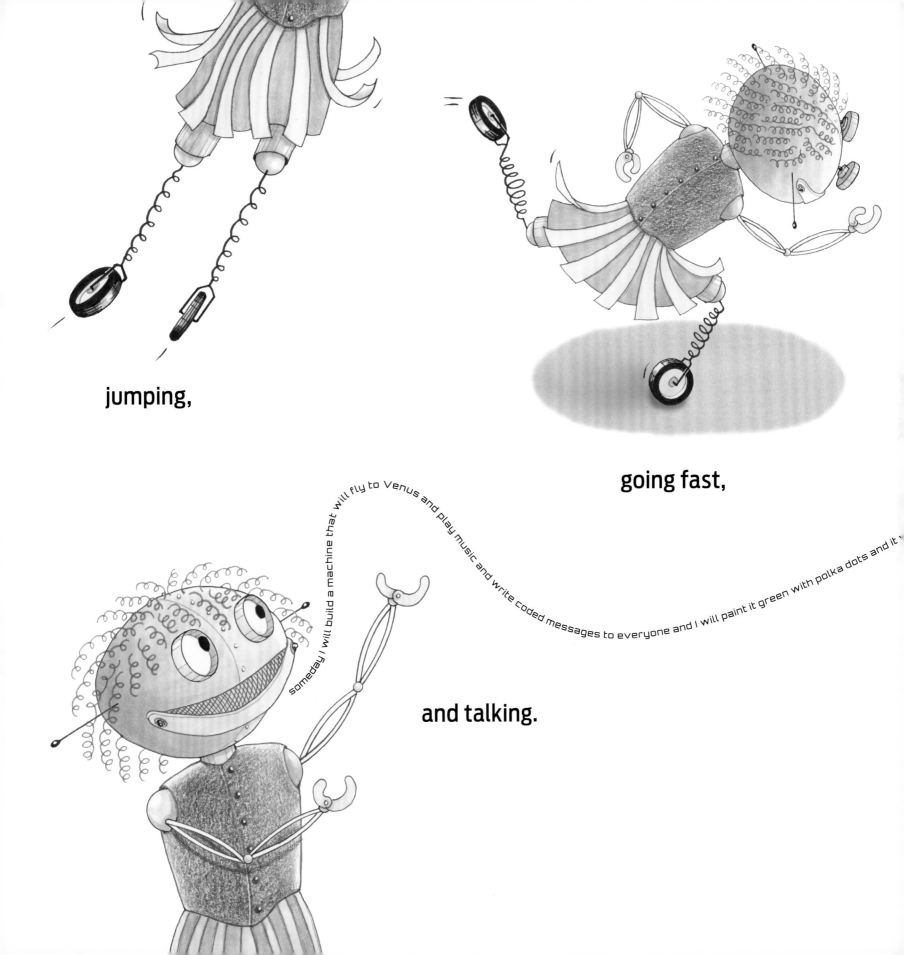

jumping,

going fast,

someday I will build a machine that will fly to Venus and play music and write coded messages to everyone and I will paint it green with polka dots and it

and talking.

One day, Betty had an idea.
"I'll build a friend!"
She started with an old
broken toaster she found
in the junk pile.

She definitely wanted a jumping friend, so she welded on some springs.

"Not now, Toby," said Betty.

She plugged in her friend, and sure enough, it jumped beautifully.

Jumping together was fun for a while, but the new friend was too slow.

"Toby, I'm busy!" said Betty.

She bolted two axles on the toaster and attached some wheels.

She added a small engine.
Now her friend would go fast!

There was just one thing left.
Betty still wanted a talking friend.
So she installed some speakers.

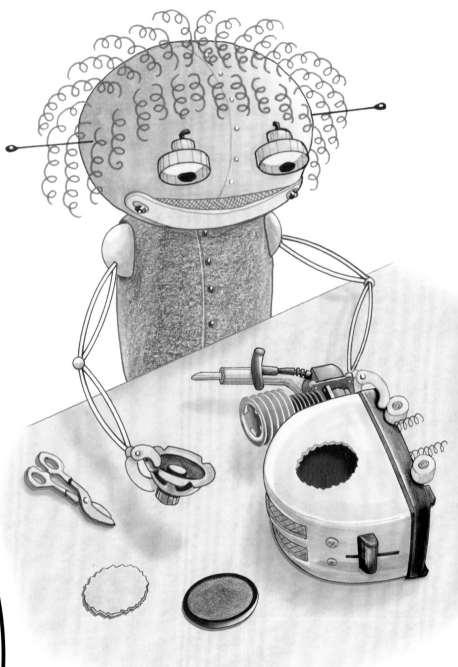

"Later, Toby, I'm almost
finished," said Betty.

But her friend was still silent.

So she attached a microphone and a recorder.

Betty rocks! I love widgets! Rivets or bolts for the new machine? Don't forget the tool kit! Let's have some crazy fun! Don't break a circuit! Don't be a rust bucket! Meet you at the junk pile!

Then she recorded some things for her friend to say.

Hooray! Her friend was finally finished! They went outside to play.

Betty's new friend could jump, go fast, and talk!

Everything was going just fine until…

... the toaster friend didn't know how to stop!
It was headed straight for Betty!

Toby zipped in front of the toaster and blocked it.

"Wow, Toby, you saved me!" said Betty.

"You got a little dinged up. Don't worry, I can fix you."

Betty repaired Toby,

and they even used some toaster parts to give him a few upgrades...

... so now he could do just about anything!

He could jump. He could run fast. And he could talk up a storm!

Betty has a new friend. And the best part?

He can also make toast!

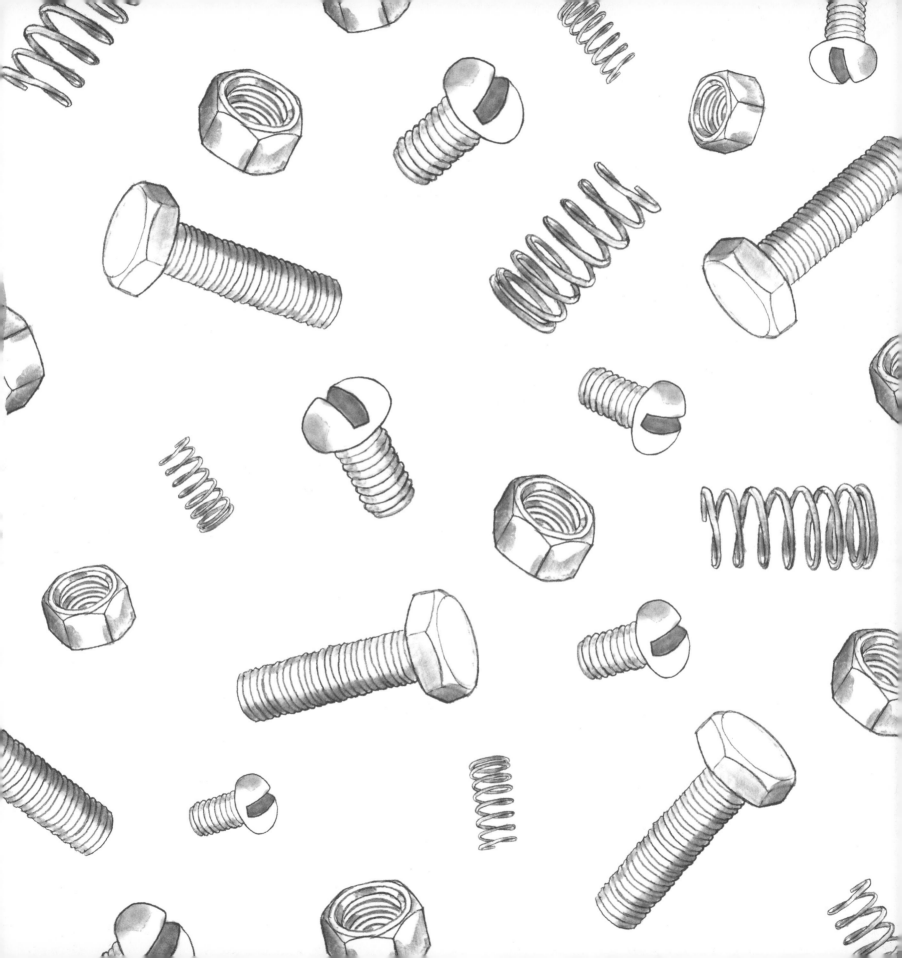

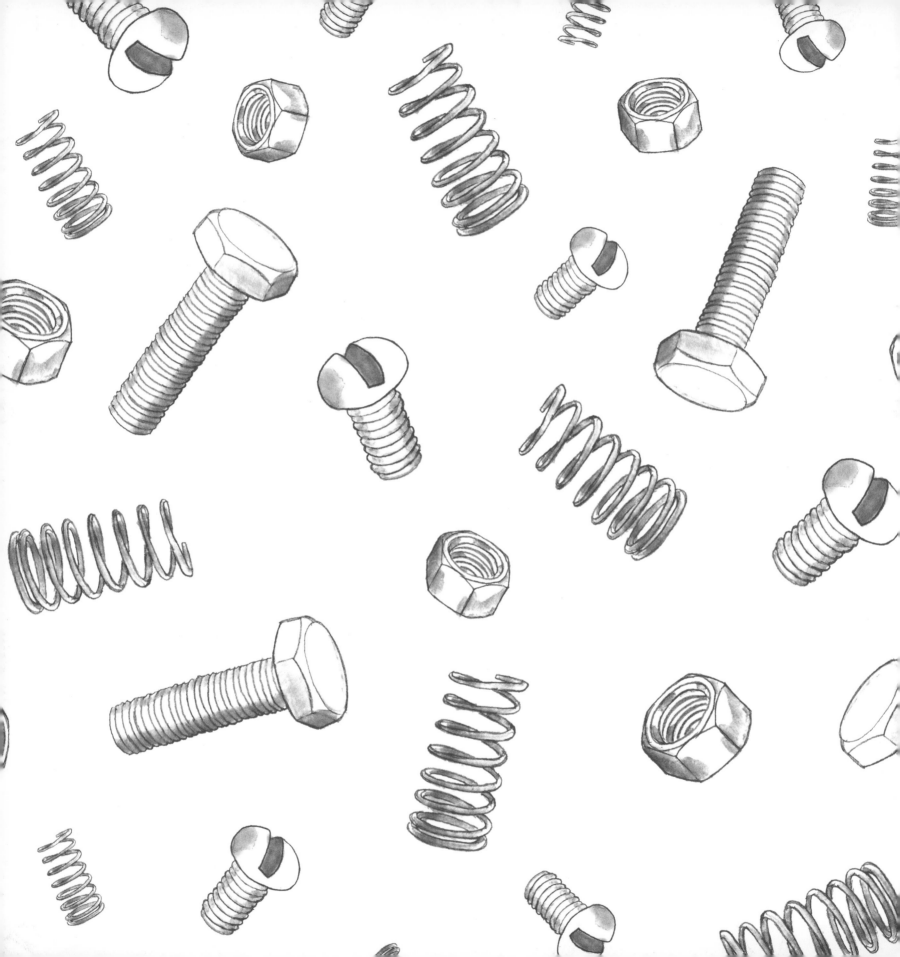